There are many children living with an alcoholic mother, father or other caregiver. This is the story of one family and how a big, stuffed, furry gorilla helped them confront the disease of alcoholism.

ISBN 0-9769460-0-9

Printed in the United States of America
Hardbound, Inc.
St. Louis, MO. 63045

Dudley

By Jackie Endraske

illustrated by Renee Nilges

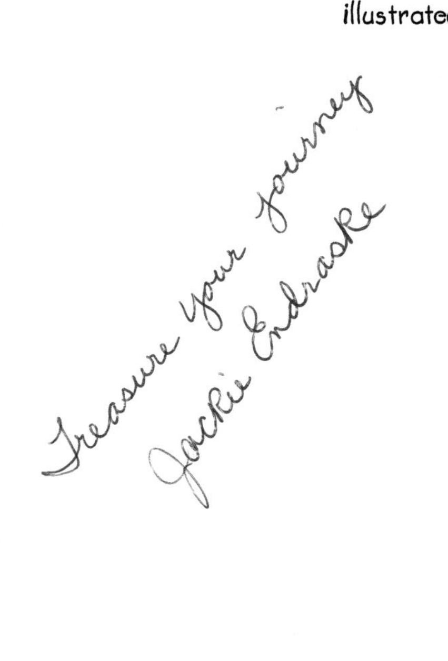

ACKNOWLEDGEMENTS

This book could not have been written without the loving support of my family and friends.

To my husband Paul, my soul mate, who has been at my side on this beautiful journey and has always encouraged me to follow my dream.

To my daughter Lori, who told me to stop sorting pantyhose and get started on this book and whose financial advice has been invaluable.

To my son Mark, whose sense of humor helped keep me on target with writing and who gave me sound business advice.

To my daughter-in-law Kathleen, who told me how necessary this book is for children living in alcoholic homes.

To Penny Holmes, whose personal request to complete this book tugged at my heart and gave me the courage to continue writing (my cheerleader).

To Pat Murphy, who has guided me through the years and taught me the meaning of living "one day at a time."

To Rose Mass, who taught me to once again believe in myself.

To Susan Willcox, whose positive outlook and caring helped me continue on the road to publication.

To the Board of Directors of FRESH Renewal Center who have been so generous with promoting Dudley.

To Karen Casey and Cheryl McKinley for their personal endorsements which truly moved me.

To Carol Martin, Dee Schroeder, Marilyn Esterline, Carol and Art Sage, Paul Endraske Jr., Ginny Dobbins, Noel Hwande and the FAB group (Linda Stewart, Mary Frances Hoffman, Mary Albrecht, Penny and Cheryl), who gave me support in countless ways.

To Alyssa Stahr, whose editing was very meaningful to the story.

To Carol and Dwight Berger for their awesome formatting and printing work.

To Renee Nilges, whose enthusiasm and belief in this project captured all of the special qualities of the characters and brought them to life.

And last but certainly not least, to Vicky Taña and Susan, who are responsible for bringing Renee and I together to fulfill my dream.

I thank you all from the bottom of my heart.

DEDICATION

To the loving memory of my mother Mary Deschu and to my dear children Mark and Lori Hertenstein. They loved me unconditionally when I couldn't love myself.

And to all children still suffering in a family with an alcoholic.

Table of Contents

Dedication 7

Chapter 1 New Friends..13

Chapter 2 Flying Away..16

Chapter 3 My New Home..23

Chapter 4 Suzyk@toystore.com..28

Chapter 5 Stuffed Animal Day..32

Chapter 6 Rock, Paper, Scissors..36

Chapter 7 Talking To Kay and Alan..43

Chapter 8 Missing Mom..50

Chapter 9 Mighty Mimi..57

Chapter 10 Acceptance..61

Chapter 11 Talking to Mother..64

Chapter 12 Freedom..69

Dudley

Chapter 1
New Friends

The most beautiful hazel eyes I had ever seen were staring at me! A little girl was standing in the mall looking at me through the toy store window. She looked so sad and worried. As I watched her, I knew I wanted to be her friend.

Her name was Kay. She was with her brother Alan and their Aunt Jenny and Uncle Bob. I overheard them talking about her eighth birthday, which was two weeks away.

"Oh Aunt Jenny, can I have the big, furry gorilla for my birthday present?" asked Kay. "He looks so warm and cuddly. He's perfect! Please, please."

Before I knew what happened, I was scooped out of the store window by Aunt

Jenny. She placed me in Kay's loving arms. Aunt Jenny paid for me and Uncle Bob said that it was time to go to the airport.

I didn't want to leave my friends in the toy store, especially Suzy Kangaroo. We always had so much fun together. But, something told me that I needed to go with Kay and her 10-year-old brother.

Tears streamed down my face as I waved goodbye to Suzy. She waved too and gave me a "thumbs-up."

I didn't know it then, but I had just started THE MOST IMPORTANT JOURNEY OF MY LIFE!

Optional Question

1. What do you think Dudley meant when he said he had just started THE MOST IMPORTANT JOURNEY OF HIS LIFE?

Chapter 2
Flying Away

After we bought Alan's favorite pizza to take with us, we dashed to the airport. Kay and Alan gave their aunt and uncle a big hug and thanked them for a wonderful week. We three "kids" boarded the airplane. This was my first time flying in a jet!

We were on our way to Sanibel Island, Florida. Alan and Kay had moved to the beach with their mother a couple of years ago after their parents' divorce. They wanted to be close to their grandmother, Mimi.

I was snuggled in Kay's arms when Alan started to tease her about me.

"Hey, what's your silly gorilla's name?" asked Alan.

"He's not silly," Kay replied. "He's very special and his name is Dudley."

"Dudley? That's a goofy name," teased Alan.

Kay's feelings were hurt and she started to cry. "It's not a goofy name. It fits him. And anyway, he's my friend! Why don't you read your book and leave me alone?" she said.

"OK, OK," Alan said.

After a few minutes he started to talk to Kay very softly.

"I'm going to miss Aunt Jenny and Uncle Bob. I wish we had told them about Mom's drinking. They've never seen how she acts when she's drunk. Maybe they could have helped," he said.

"Yeah," said Kay unhappily. "I hate keeping this secret. I don't want to have my friends over. I never know what she'll be doing." She paused and then continued, "Oh, my tummy is starting to hurt again."

After awhile Alan started to read his book again and Kay fell asleep, using me as a pillow.

As we flew over the island, the beautiful, blue ocean and white sand looked quiet and peaceful. I had heard about all of the unusual shells on the island. I thought about how cool it would be to play on the beach and collect them. It looked like an awesome place to live.

Soon Alan poked Kay and said, "Wake up, we're landing. I hope Mom's here to meet us."

"Me too. She's always late for everything," answered Kay.

Mother waited at the gate for them. They ran to her and we all had a big group hug and lots of kisses.

"Yuck, she smells like she's been drinking," I said to myself. I knew Alan and Kay noticed too, because they gave each other a worried look.

"Oh my! Who is this?" asked Mother as she pointed to me.

Kay answered, "This is Dudley. He's an early birthday present from Aunt Jenny and Uncle Bob."

"How ya doing Mom? Did you miss us? What did you do while we were gone?" asked Alan.

Mother said, "I caught up with a lot of school stuff during spring break like lesson plans and grading papers. But, I missed you both so much. I'm really glad you're home."

After we got our luggage, we started for my new home. We had to drive over a two-lane causeway to the island.

At times, Mother weaved across the center line. Kay hugged me so I wouldn't fall off her lap and Alan clutched the pizza.

I could tell they were both scared. Alan teased Kay to try to get her mind off their mother's driving.

"Give me that silly looking gorilla. I'll use him for a punching bag," he said.

"Stop it! Stop it! He's my special friend!" yelled Kay.

Mother screamed, "You're both making me nervous! Five minutes of quiet time! If I hear one more sound, you'll both be grounded from TV for a week!"

Alan and Kay didn't say another word.

Optional Questions

1. Why do you think Kay and Alan didn't tell their aunt and uncle about their mother's drinking problem?

2. Have you ever been in a car with someone who had been drinking? If so, how did you feel?

Chapter 3

My New Home

When we got to their condo, the kids took their suitcases upstairs. I was left in the family room and saw Mother sneak a large glass of alcohol.

Kay came back downstairs to get me. She saw Mother put the liquor bottle under the sink. After she picked me up, we went to her room. She buried her face into my fur and cried.

Alan heard her crying and tiptoed into her room. He put his arm around her and hugged her.

"I wish Mom wouldn't drink anymore," sobbed Kay.

"I know," said Alan quietly. "She keeps promising us she will stop. I wonder if it's our fault? Maybe it's something we're doing. Maybe we shouldn't leave her alone."

As I listened to them I really wanted to help, but I didn't know how. I needed to talk to my friend Suzy Kangaroo. We always talked about our problems and tried to help each other. But, I was afraid someone would hear me if I called her on the phone. I finally decided to e-mail her after everyone went to sleep.

Mother heated the pizza in the oven. After saying grace she started to eat, but Alan and Kay just looked at their pizza.

Mother asked, "Why aren't you eating? This is from your favorite pizza place."

"I'm not very hungry," answered Alan.

"My tummy hurts," said Kay.

"Kay must have been thinking about her mother's drinking because her tummy was hurting again," I thought. "This had happened on the airplane, too."

"Well then, forget about dessert," snapped Mother.

"What's for dessert?" asked Alan. "You hardly ever cook anymore. We just eat pizza, hamburgers or frozen dinners. All you care about is drinking, drinking, drinking."

He started to yell, "When you hugged us at the airport we could smell booze on your breath! We could have had a terrible accident today!"

"I feel horrible about that. I didn't drink that much and I'm trying to stop, really I am!" cried Mother.

"I think you drank a lot before we got home!" screamed Alan. "Just stop!"

"I want to, but I don't know how," said Mother very softly.

"It's simple, just don't drink!" said Alan disgustedly.

"It's not that easy, but I promise I won't drink anymore. I'm really scared. Now just leave me alone and do your homework. Spring break is over and we all have school tomorrow," said Mother.

They had a very quiet evening. Mother graded her school papers and Kay and Alan finished their homework. They all went to bed early.

Optional Questions

1. Mother promised she wouldn't drink anymore. Did your loved one ever promise you he or she wouldn't drink again?
2. Did he or she keep his or her promise?
3. How did it make you feel?

Chapter 4

Suzyk@toystore.com

When all was quiet, I crept downstairs to the computer. I was glad I had watched Alan doing his homework on it earlier. It was as easy to use as the one at the toy store.

Suzyk@toystore.com

Hey Suzy,

I really miss you. I'm on an island close to Florida. The kids are upset because their mother drinks a lot. They are wondering if it's their fault. Maybe she is an alcoholic like our store manager. I don't know what to do. Please help!

Love, Dudley

While I was waiting for her answer I fell asleep. I woke up about two hours later and saw her message.

AlanKay@SanIs.com

Hi Dudley,

I miss you too. Sorry to hear about their mother. This sounds very serious. They need a friend. Talk to them. Let me know how it goes.

Love, Suzy

Immediately I wrote:

Suzyk@toystore.com

Thanks Suzy.

I knew I could count on you. I'll talk to Kay and Alan soon. Keep us in your prayers.

Love, Dudley

I felt better and checked on Alan in his room. He wasn't there and I found him in Kay's room. They had both fallen asleep in the beanbag chair. I snuggled between them and fell asleep.

Optional Questions

1. Dudley e-mailed Suzy about the family problem. Do you have someone to talk to when you are sad, angry, lonely or confused?

2. If so, how does this person help you?

Chapter 5

Stuffed Animal Day

The next morning everyone rushed around getting ready for school. It was "Bring Your Favorite Stuffed Animal to School Day" and I was going with them!

Soon I was on my very first school bus ride. All the kids except for Kay and Alan were talking and acting silly with their friends. They both seemed very sad.

When we got to school they walked slowly to their classrooms. Alan dragged his book bag and Kay clutched me in her arms.

Sharing time was first on the schedule in Kay's class. Her teacher called the students one-by-one to come to the front of the classroom. Every student shared why their stuffed animal was special to them.

Emma said she liked to set up a zoo with all her animals. The baby giraffe was Emma's favorite because it could see so far and watch over her. Ben liked the cheetah because it was the fastest animal. He took it to all his baseball games to remind him to charge around the bases. Brian and Abby liked to

cuddle with their favorite soft animal while they were sleeping.

When it was Kay's turn, she was choking back the tears and held me close to her heart. She said I helped her when she was sad and lonely. It made me feel warm inside to know that Kay loved me that much.

I sat next to her during math class. Everyone worked very quietly. Instead of doing the problems, Kay looked out the window. She couldn't concentrate on her worksheet.

At lunch Kay handed me over to Alan for the afternoon. I went to PE class with him. All the kids were sitting in a circle listening to the teacher. Alan was giggling and poking the boy next to him.

"Alan, please keep your hands to yourself and pay attention," said his teacher. When he continued to play around his teacher asked him to see her after class.

Alan and his teacher talked quietly after the other students went back to class. "Alan, you usually listen in class. Is something bothering you?" asked the teacher.

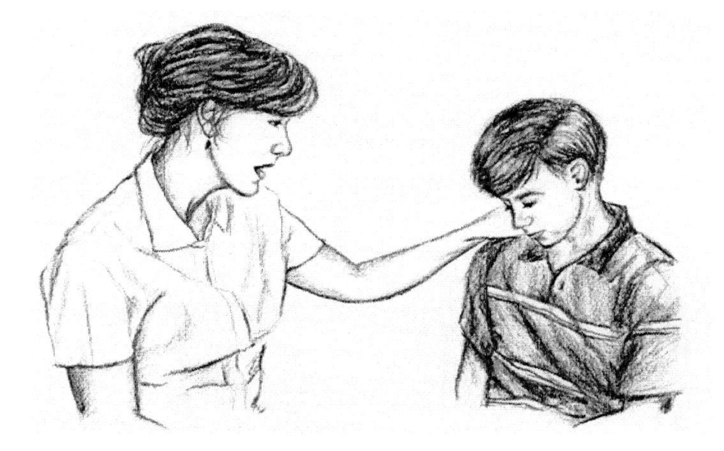

"No," answered Alan while looking down at the floor.

I wanted to poke him and tell him to talk to her. But, I didn't want to scare him. It was important to tell him that I could talk when we were alone. Kay, Alan and I had to talk that night!

Optional Question

1. Kay and Alan had difficulty paying attention in school. Does this ever happen to you?

Chapter 6

Rock, Paper, Scissors

After school I watched Alan and Kay doing their homework in the kitchen while Mother put the groceries away.

"Mom seems OK today," whispered Kay to Alan.

"Yeah, you never know from day to day," answered Alan in a whisper.

"What are you two whispering about?" asked Mother.

"Nothing," they answered.

"I'm really tired and have a lot to do tonight," said Mother. "Let's go out for supper."

Alan remembered the scary ride home from the airport the day before. He hesitated and then said, "OK, I guess so."

"Dudley goes where I go, OK?" asked Kay.

"Sounds good," said Mother.

"I get the front seat," teased Kay as she ran to the car.

"No way!" yelled Alan. "You just want to play your CD's. It's my turn."

"Mom, he's telling stories. It's my turn!" screamed Kay.

"Both of you settle down right now!" shouted Mom.

"OK, OK. Let's play rock, paper, scissors to see who gets to sit in the front," suggested Alan.

I noticed that Mother was getting very crabby.

"Why do you two always have to play that silly game?" asked Mother.

"You're no fun anymore! What's the matter with you?" asked Alan. "Why are you so cranky?"

"Just get in the car!" screamed Mother.

"Wow, is it always like this?" I wondered.

We had a quiet ride to the restaurant. No one said anything during dinner. I looked around at the other families. They were all laughing and joking with each other. I saw Kay and Alan sadly looking at the other families too.

Everyone was quiet on the way home, too. Mother suggested that we watch a movie. She must have felt bad about screaming at the kids.

We watched the movie in the family room. From where I was sitting I could see Mother sneak a drink of alcohol in the kitchen.

"Hey, do you guys want some popcorn and soda?" asked Mother as she stepped into the family room.

"That sounds cool," said Kay.

"I'm really thirsty," said Alan.

"This sure was a good idea," said Kay.

FRESH
HOT
PIZZA

"I'm really thirsty. It must be the popcorn. I need some more soda," said Mother as she went into the kitchen again.

When she returned to the family room she lost her balance and almost knocked a lamp off the table. Kay looked panicked. Alan just rolled his eyes in disgust.

Then he started to scream at his mother.

"You've been drinking again!" he screamed.

"No I haven't!" yelled Mother.

"Let me smell your soda!" Alan demanded.

"No! Don't you believe me?" asked Mother.

"Not anymore! Why should I trust you! Just last night you promised AGAIN that you would stop drinking!" yelled Alan.

"Stop it, stop it!" screamed Kay as she held me tightly.

Alan grabbed the drink out of Mother's hand, spilled part of it and then smelled it.

"Just like I said! You've been drinking all night!" exclaimed Alan.

"I just needed a couple of drinks to calm down. It was a rough day at school. And anyway I can stop whenever I want to," sobbed Mother.

"Yeah, yeah, right!" yelled Alan. "Don't **EVER** say that again unless you really mean it!"

He stomped up the stairs to his room and slammed the door. I could hear him throwing things.

Optional Questions

1. Look at the picture of the restaurant again. Do you ever feel this alone with your family?

2. What began as a family fun night didn't turn out that way. Has this ever happened to your family?

Chapter 7
Talking To Kay and Alan

Kay picked me up and ran upstairs to her room. She squeezed me so hard that I could hardly breathe. This seemed like the perfect time to talk to her.

"Kay, please don't be scared. I can talk. Only my friends at the toy store and kids can hear me," I said.

She looked at me with those big hazel eyes. When she tried to speak no words would come out.

"I'm your friend. I feel that you chose me for a reason ---- to help you and Alan," I said.

"How can you talk?" Kay finally asked. "You aren't real."

"I'm real to children and stuffed animals. They're the only ones who can hear me and talk to me," I explained.

"We don't need any help. We're fine," she said.

"You and Alan aren't fine. You're both always afraid of what your mother is going to say and do. You know that your mother drinks too much. It looks like she has a problem with alcohol," I said.

I continued, "She acts like the owner of the toy store where you first saw me. He drank a lot and didn't want anyone to know how much he was drinking. He finally admitted that he was an alcoholic. Maybe your mother is an alcoholic too."

"What's an alcoholic?" Kay asked.

At that moment Alan came bursting into Kay's room.

"Who are you talking to?" he asked.

"I'm talking to Dudley," Kay answered.

"Oh yeah, right! You're trying to tell me your big gorilla is talking to you!" Alan said

I had to say something. "Alan, please don't make fun of Kay," I said. "Don't be frightened. I can talk. I think Kay brought me here so I could help you two."

"Wow, I must be dreaming," whispered Alan. "How can you talk to us?"

"I don't know. One day in the toy store I asked my friend Suzy Kangaroo a question. A little boy holding Suzy answered me! Then he and I started to talk to each other. That's how I found out," I explained.

"Wow, this is so weird and at the same time it's so cool." said Alan in amazement. "What were you and Kay talking about?"

"I was just telling Kay that I know someone who has a problem with drinking like your mother," I said.

"Our mother doesn't have a problem," said Alan.

"I think your mother might be an alcoholic because she drinks too much," I explained. "Then she starts to act weird. This happens a lot. It's a disease and it's called alcoholism."

"Even though she wants to stop, she can't. Once she takes the first drink her body wants more," I said.

"My mom isn't sick. She can't be an alcoholic. She's not of one those bums who sits on the street corner drinking out of a paper bag!" yelled Alan as he ran out of the room.

Optional Questions

1. Read the last two paragraphs again. Do you think your loved one is an alcoholic?

2. What does this mean to you?

Chapter 8
Missing Mom

I tucked Kay's blanket around her and told her that I would stay with her.

"We've talked enough for tonight. It's been a rough couple of days. Time to get some sleep," I said.

"I wish Mom would tuck me in like she used to. I miss her," sobbed Kay.

I tried to calm her and said, "I know she loves you Kay. But, when she's drinking that's all she can think about."

After she fell asleep I decided to e-mail Suzy.

Suzyk@toystore.com

Hey Suzy,

I talked to the kids about their mother tonight. Alan is angry and doesn't believe me. Kay is confused. I just need to talk.

Miss you, Dudley

Suzy must have been typing on the computer because she replied immediately.

AlanKay@SanIs.com

Hi Dudley,

They sound pretty normal to me. They don't want to believe their mother has a problem with alcohol. Good thing you are there to help them through this. Give them time to think about what you have told them. Let's keep in touch. I'll keep all of you in my prayers.

Love, Suzy

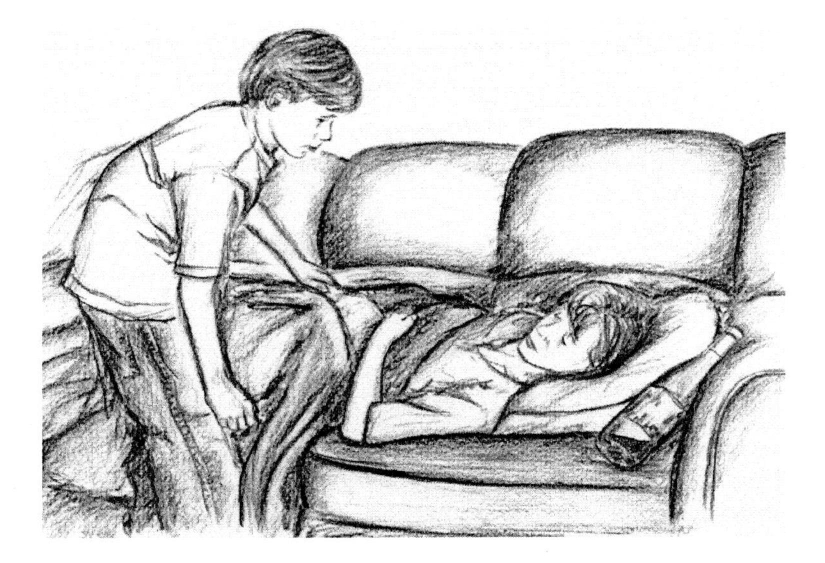

I fell asleep in the family room. I heard Alan come downstairs a couple of hours later. He found his mother passed out on the couch. A wine bottle was on the couch beside her. He gently put a blanket over her.

With tears in his eyes he said, "I love you Mom. Please get better. I miss you so much and I need you."

Mother didn't feel well the next morning. She had a stomachache and a headache. But, she went to school anyway.

Since it was such a beautiful day Alan wanted all of us to go to the beach after school. It was as awesome as I had dreamed it would be. The waves were gently rolling in, leaving many shells behind. Two rolled right into my paw. It was so peaceful.

For a while Alan and Kay played in the waves, splashing and tossing a beachball back and forth. Later they collected shells and made sand castles. All this time Mother lay asleep in a beach chair.

And me, well, it gave me a good feeling to see Kay and Alan having fun. But, I was worried about their mother.

I overheard Kay and Alan talking.

"Mom sure is quiet. I miss playing with her on the beach. I guess she isn't feeling too good. Why does she drink so much?" asked Kay.

"I don't know. Maybe Dudley is right about Mom," said Alan.

On the way home Mother told them that she had been doing a lot of thinking. She was **REALLY** going to stop drinking this time.

Kay and Alan didn't say anything. They had heard this before and they didn't want to get in an argument.

Optional Questions

1. Explain the title, "Missing Mom". How could they miss Mom when they lived with her?

2. Have you ever had to take care of your loved one?

Chapter 9

Mighty Mimi

When we got home I met Mimi, Kay and Alan's grandmother. She was little, but mighty! She said that she had tried to call them all day. I then realized that Mimi was also worried about her daughter and grandchildren. Mimi and Mother started to talk.

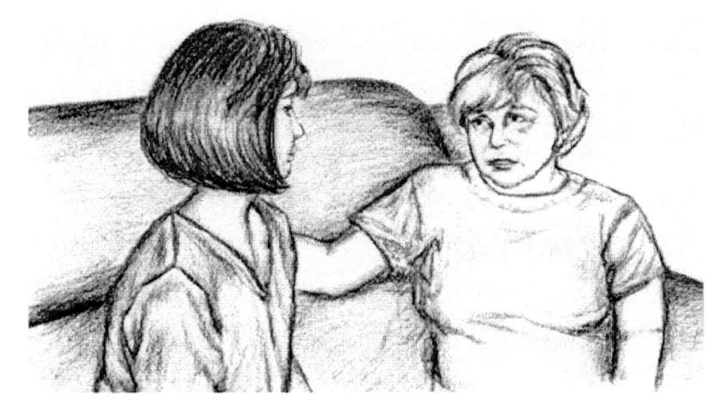

"You look terrible. Were you drinking again last night?" asked Mimi.

"No, I'm just tired," sighed Mother.

"I don't believe you," said Mimi. You always say you're tired. I think you are drinking so much that you're all worn out. You've just got to STOP! You have these two wonderful children to take care of!"

"I'm not drinking that much. I'm going to stop, really I am. Why don't you just mind your own business and go home!" yelled Mother.

"I'm not going to leave! I'm going to cook dinner so my grandchildren eat a good home-cooked meal tonight," said Mimi.

It was very quiet during dinner. As she was leaving, Mimi told the kids to call her if they needed her.

Before they went to bed, Kay and Alan told me that they wanted to help their mother. But, they didn't know what to do. I suggested we all pray about it. We knelt by Alan's bed and prayed.

Kay prayed, "Dear God, please help my mommy to stop drinking."

"Dear God, I'm so angry. I don't know what to do anymore. Please help us," prayed Alan.

I prayed, "Please show us how to help their mother."

Mother came in and kissed them goodnight, then she went downstairs. I followed her and hid behind the chair in the family room. I overheard her talking to herself.

"I've got so much work to do. I'm really feeling stressed out. A drink would sure help. But, I did promise the kids that I would stop. I love them so much and I want to be a good mom. I'll have just ONE drink and I'll quit TOMORROW," she said.

I watched her drink and I wanted to yell at her to stop, but I knew it wouldn't do any good. She couldn't hear me. I decided to e-mail Suzy again.

Suzyk@toystore.com

Hi Suzy,

I'm really frustrated. The kids and their grandmother are starting to believe Mother has a problem. I think they're all getting to the point of doing something about it. The kids and I prayed tonight. Miss you.

Love, Dudley

Suzy responded quickly.

AlanKay@SanIs.com

Hey,

Sounds like you're helping a lot. The kids are listening to you and talking. It's time to do something. You're all in my prayers. Miss you too.

Love, Suzy

Optional Questions

1. Why does Mother lie to her mother about her drinking?
2. Do you think that Mother wanted to stop drinking?

Chapter 10
Acceptance

When the alarm went off the next morning, Alan and Kay went downstairs and tried to awaken Mother. She said that she had the flu and couldn't go to school. They didn't believe her, but they got dressed, ate breakfast and then went to school.

Instead of going home after school, they walked to Mimi's house to talk to her.

"Mimi, Mom didn't go to work again today. She said it was the flu, but we saw another empty bottle," cried Alan. "We don't know what to do."

Mimi took Alan and Kay into her arms and told them that she thought they should talk to their minister.

She called her daughter and told her the kids had stopped by for a snack after school.

Then she called their minister, Reverend Long. They went to see him and told him about their family problem.

Reverend Long said, "I'm glad you all came today. You must all love her very much. But, I'm sure you don't like her right now. From what you have told me it sounds like she is an alcoholic. When she says she will stop drinking she really means it. But, as soon as she takes the first drink, it's hard to stop."

He continued, "You must all remember that you haven't done anything to make her drink. She needs to admit to herself that she needs help. All of you need to tell her how you feel. We need to practice what we're going to say to her. After that we all need to talk to her together."

That night Mimi talked to Mother about all of them going back to church. She thought they should talk to their minister. I guess Mother was feeling so bad about her drinking that she agreed.

Optional Questions

1. How do you think Kay and Alan felt when they went to talk to their grandmother about their mother's drinking problem?

2. Do you know that it's okay not to like your alcoholic loved one when they are drinking?

Chapter 11
Talking to Mother

The next day we were all in Reverend Long's study. The minister started to talk to Mother.

"I'm happy you all want to come back to church. But, that isn't the real reason we are meeting today," he said.

He looked at Mother and said, "Everyone is concerned about your drinking. Your family would like to tell you how they feel when you drink."

Mother listened very carefully as each person spoke.

Tearfully Kay told her, "When you drink, I feel like you don't love me anymore. My tummy hurts a lot."

"I'm really mad at you when you're drinking. I don't want to fight anymore. I want us to do things as a family again," said Alan.

With tears in her eyes, Mimi looked at her daughter and said, "I worry about you and the children. I feel so helpless. When you're drinking I feel like we're losing you. We love you so much."

After a few minutes Reverend Long said, "I hear everyone say that they want you to stop drinking. Your mother is worried about all of you. Your children can't depend on you and are scared."

With tears rolling down her cheeks Mother said, "I don't see how you all can still love me. I feel that I have pushed you all away. I want to stop drinking, but I don't know how."

"There is a way," explained Reverend Long. "Alcoholics Anonymous has helped millions of people. Alcoholism is a disease. An alcoholic can't stop with just one drink. One drink leads to another and another until the alcoholic is drunk. Being an alcoholic doesn't mean you are a weak or a bad person."

He continued, "But, everyone must decide for themselves if he or she is an alcoholic. People in AA help each other stay sober ONE DAY AT A TIME. If you really want to stop drinking, they can help you too."

Mother said, "I don't know. I just don't know if I'm an alcoholic. Some days I think I can stop drinking. Other days I don't know if I can stop. I've tried so many times and haven't been able to stop. Maybe I'm having a hard time because it is a disease. One drink always leads to more drinks." She slowly walked out of the room looking sad and confused.

Everyone was surprised that Mother left, except Reverend Long. He said, "Don't be discouraged. At least she listened. We've done everything we can do. Now, it's up to HER."

Optional Questions

1. Do you think it took a lot of courage for Kay, Alan and Mimi to talk to Mother?

2. Can you explain why alcoholism is called a disease?

Chapter 12

Freedom

During the next week Kay, Alan and Mimi tried to go about their daily lives. They thought about Mother a lot. They tried not to watch her all the time, but it was hard.

Mother didn't drink. No one knew it, but she was afraid to pick up that "FIRST DRINK".

On Saturday afternoon they were celebrating Kay's eighth birthday. Kay's friends and Mimi were there. All of the kids had a great time, except for Kay and Alan. No one but Mimi and I noticed the sad look in their eyes as Kay opened her gifts. After that they all played games and ate cake and ice cream. Mother acted as if everything was fine.

Mother made it through the party without taking a drink. As Mother was cleaning the kitchen after the party she said quietly, "A glass of wine would sure taste good right now." Then she looked terrified.

She remembered the look of pain on the faces of her family that day in Reverend Long's study. Mother also remembered their sad words.

"I'm afraid to take a drink. I know that one drink will lead to more drinks. Once I start I know I won't be able to stop. I'll either get drunk or pass out," sobbed Mother.

She continued to cry, "Maybe I am an alcoholic. I can't do this by myself. I'm so scared. I want to be a sober mother. I know I need HELP."

That afternoon Mother went to her first Alcoholics Anonymous meeting. When it was her turn to speak she was finally able to say:

"I'm an alcoholic, and I need help."

This is not the end of this story,

it is just . . .

A NEW BEGINNING

Mother went to a lot of AA meetings and began to understand about the disease of alcoholism. The family started talking more and having fun together. They all went to an AA picnic where they met some of Mother's new friends. It took time, but little by little they became a family again . . .

ONE DAY AT A TIME

Dear Friend,

If you are living in an alcoholic home there is help for you, too. Find a special, cuddly soft animal (real or stuffed) to snuggle.

Talk to a grown-up you trust about the problem. The person you choose may be a family member, a teacher, a counselor or a special friend.

YOU ARE NOT ALONE

OPTIONAL ACTIVITIES and QUESTIONS

1. Why was it hard for Mother to admit that she <u>is</u> an alcoholic?

2. Draw a picture of yourself and your loved one when he or she is <u>not</u> drinking.

3. How do you feel when this person is <u>not</u> drinking?

4. Draw a picture of yourself and your loved one when he or she <u>is</u> drinking.

5. How do you feel when this person <u>is</u> drinking?

ABOUT THE AUTHOR

Jackie Endraske is a retired elementary school teacher. For many years she had wanted to write a children's book about Dudley. He had been given to her daughter Lori and later lived in Jackie's fourth grade classroom.

While there Dudley was loved by the students and was in great demand as a silent reading buddy. Jackie noticed that he was especially comforting to those children living in homes of alcoholics. The disease of alcoholism and Dudley became entwined as she started to write this story.

Jackie has a Bachelor of Science in Education from the University of Missouri and a Masters degree in Education from Kent State. She has been a member of the Society of Children's Book Writers and Illustrators (SCBWI) since 2003.

Dudley is her first children's book.
www.dudleythegorilla.com

ABOUT THE ILLUSTRATOR

Renee Nilges is an award-winning artist who paints and creates from what moves her. When asked how long she's been painting, she says, "Art has been a part of my life for as long as I can remember."

She has been self-employed as a freelance artist, selling her paintings and commissioned work since 1998.

She has a background in commercial art, but is mostly self taught in fine art. Renee's work is in collections nationwide as well as abroad. She is a member of the National Oil and Acrylic Painter's Society (NOAPS). Her work is represented by the Manitou Gallery in California, Missouri and The Dunklin Street Gallery in Jefferson City, Missouri.

You may find more of Renee's work on her Web site at:
www.reneesartwork.com